WILLIAM AND BOOMER

by Lindsay Barrett George

Greenwillow Books
New York

For my parents

Watercolors, dyes, and colored
pencils were used for the
full-color illustrations.
The text type is Goudy Old Style.

Copyright © 1987 by Lindsay Barrett George
All rights reserved. No part of this book
may be reproduced without permission
in writing from Greenwillow Books,
105 Madison Avenue, New York, N.Y. 10016.
Printed in Hong Kong by South China Printing Co.

First Edition   10 9 8 7 6 5 4 3 2 1

Library of Congress Cataloging-in-Publication Data
George, Lindsay Barrett.   William and Boomer.
Summary: Young William longs to swim like his new pet
goose, and as the summer passes he learns to do just that.
[1. Geese—Fiction. 2. Swimming] I. Title.
PZ7.G29334Wi   1987   [E]   86-9789
ISBN 0-688-06640-2   ISBN 0-688-06641-0 (lib. bdg.)

William lived with his parents by a lake in the woods. He loved to go fishing with his father. One spring morning they spotted a fuzzy yellow ball moving in the reeds.
It was a baby goose.

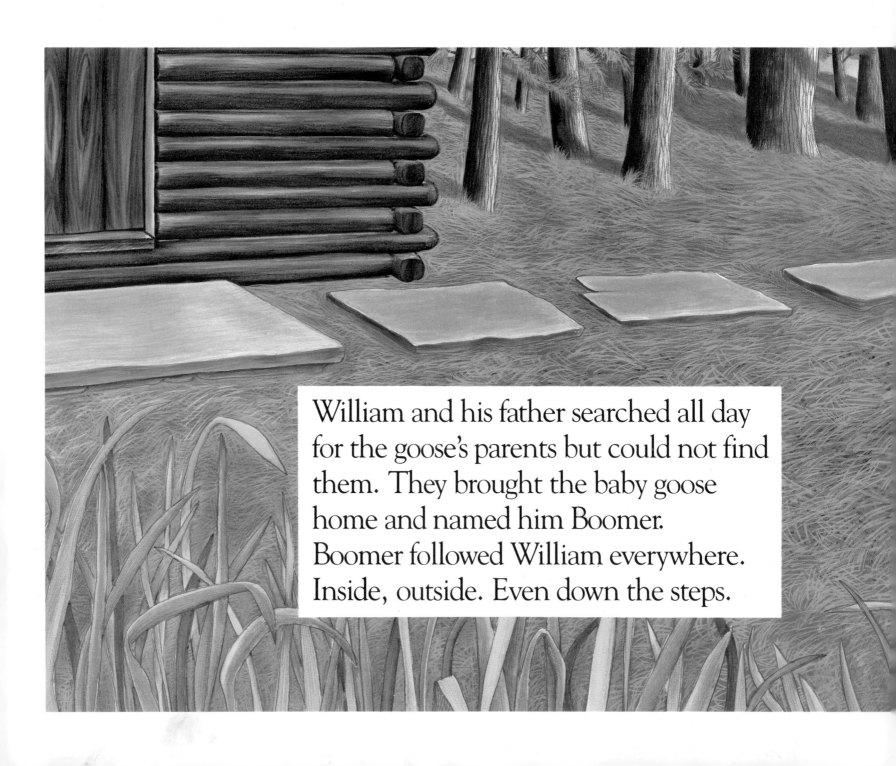

William and his father searched all day
for the goose's parents but could not find
them. They brought the baby goose
home and named him Boomer.
Boomer followed William everywhere.
Inside, outside. Even down the steps.

Boomer loved to swim.
"Can I learn to swim, too?"
asked William.

"Not until the water is warmer," said his mother.

Some days William and Boomer
searched for turtles along the shore.

And other days they spent their afternoons sunbathing on the dock.

When William and his father went
fishing, Boomer followed the canoe.
"Now can I learn to swim?" asked
William.
"Not until the water's a little warmer,"
said his father.

As spring turned to summer, Boomer grew. And so did William. He learned to paddle a canoe and tie it to the dock.

He learned how to unhook a fish
and skip stones across the lake.

"Is the water warmer now?" William asked.
"Yes!" said his parents.
William and his father walked down to the lake.

First he learned to hold his breath under water.

Then he learned to float and kick.
Then stroke with his arms.

And one day he could swim!
William and Boomer swam together
every day the whole summer long.

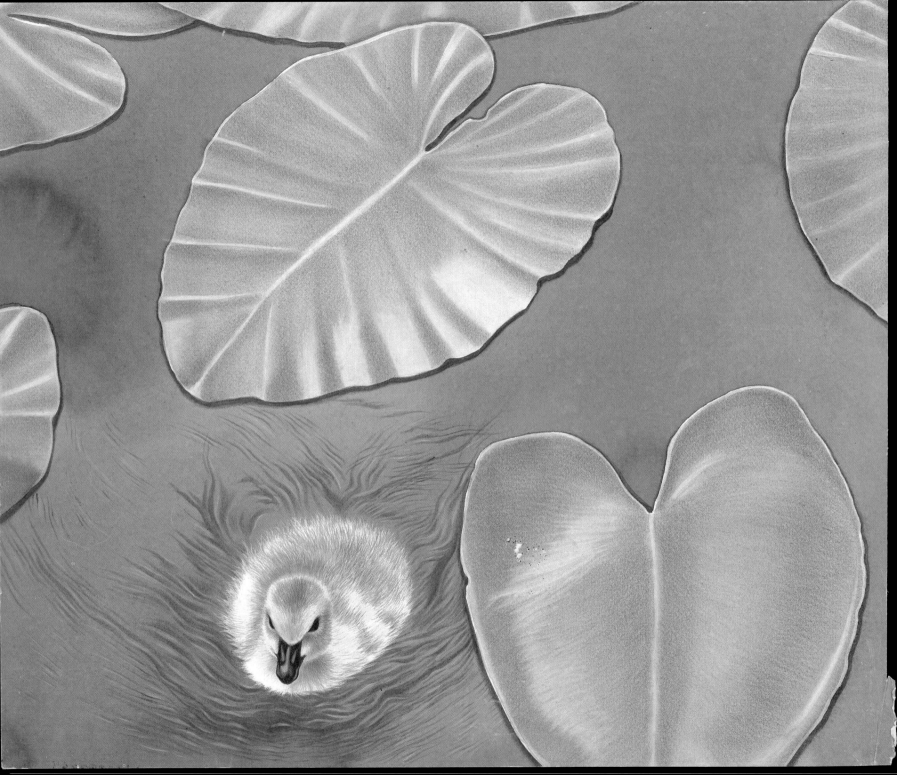